BULLFROG GROWS UP

BULLFROG GROWS UP

BY ROSAMOND DAUER
ILLUSTRATED BY BYRON BARTON

Greenwillow
Read-alone

GREENWILLOW BOOKS
A Division of William Morrow & Company, Inc./New York

Library of Congress Cataloging in Publication Data
Dauer, Rosamond. Bullfrog grows up. (Read-alone)
Summary: A family of mice raises a card-playing, bath-taking tadpole who as a bullfrog begins to eat alarming amounts.   [1. Animals—Fiction]   I. Barton, Byron.   II. Title.   PZ7. D2615BU
    [E]   75-19097   ISBN 0-688-80020-3   ISBN 0-688-84020-5 Lib. bdg.

FOR CHRIS AND MATT

One spring day
Chris and Matt
went to a pond
near their home
to catch a tadpole.

They found one swimming
in the muddy water.

He said,

"I am all by myself.

May I come home with you?"

So Chris and Matt
took him home
in a bucket.

Mother said,
"Isn't he nice!
He is very small."

Father said,
"He will grow up
to be a bullfrog.
He's going to be big."

And Father was right.

Bullfrog grew and grew.

He became so big
that Chris and Matt
put him in the bathtub.

After a while, he didn't
have a tail anymore.
He grew feet instead.
Very big feet.

His feet meant he could follow
Chris and Matt around
and do all the things
they liked to do.

Chris and Matt taught Bullfrog
how to play cards.
He liked that very much.

He especially liked to play
Go Fish.

He also liked to eat.
One day he popped
out of the bathtub
after a relaxing bath
and said,

"I feel hungry.

How about a hamburger

with relish?"

"Okay," said Chris and Matt.

And they asked Mother
for three hamburgers
with relish.

Mother didn't ask any questions.
Not then.

But soon she wondered.
Where was all the food
she had bought?

It was all gone!

She went looking for Bullfrog.
He was sitting on the porch
in the sun.
"Have you been eating
all my food?" she asked.

"Indeed I have,"
said Bullfrog.
"I am a growing frog."
"You sure are," said Mother.

And Bullfrog grew and grew
and was very comfortable
living with Chris and Matt
and Mother and Father.

But one night,
after a fierce pillow fight
with Chris and Matt,

when Father was almost
completely covered with feathers,
Father said,

"What kind of a bullfrog
is this?
He eats hamburgers,
has pillow fights,
and plays cards all day."

No one could think
of anything to say,
except Bullfrog.

"I love all of you,"
he said.
"You are my family."

Chris and Matt said,
"And we love you too, Bullfrog.
You are the best card player
we know."

And that was the end of that.

Until the next day.

When Father came home
the next afternoon,
there was Bullfrog

sitting in Father's chair,
reading Father's newspaper,
and wearing Father's slippers.

Father sat down
next to Bullfrog.
"The time has come,"
he said to Bullfrog,
"to talk about you."

"Who, me?"
asked Bullfrog.
"Yes, you," said Father.

"It is time to be thinking
of your own Frog Family.
You are grown up now."
"I am at that,"
said Bullfrog.

"The bathtub *and* your chair
are getting a little small.
But how can I leave you?"
asked Bullfrog.
"I am happy here."

Chris and Matt and Mother
put their arms around
Bullfrog.
"We have been happy too,"
they said.
"But you are too big for us.
You must find a place
for yourself in the world."

Bullfrog thought
about it.
"I shall need lunch,"
he said.

"Yes," said Mother.

"And a pack of cards,"
   said Bullfrog.

"Yes," said Chris and Matt.

"And a last bath,"
   said Bullfrog.

"Yes," said Father.

So Bullfrog took his bath,

packed up his lunch,

and picked up

his deck of cards.

"I am off to find

a very big lake,"

he said.

"I will start

my *own* family."

"We will miss you,"
    said Father.
"We will think of you often,"
    said Chris and Matt.
"I will never forget you,"
    said Mother.
"Of course you will miss me,"
    said Bullfrog.
"But you will hear from me
    every spring
    in frog-talk.
    It will always mean
    I love you."

53

So they kissed Bullfrog,
and he went down the road
waving good-bye and
practicing his frog-talk.